Clarinet Exam Pack

ABRSM Grade 4

Selected from the 2018–2021 syllabus

Name

Date of exam

Contents

page

Consultant Editor for ABRSM: David Blackwell
Footnotes: Dominic Wells

Other pieces for Grade 4

LIST A

4 **Bizet** Chanson bohème (from *Carmen*), arr. Lawrance. *Great Winners for Clarinet* (Brass Wind)
5 **Dvořák** Humoresque, Op. 101 No. 7, arr. Birtel. *Classical Music for Children for Clarinet* (Schott)
6 **Mendelssohn** Song Without Words, Op. 67 No. 2, arr. King & Frank. *Mendelssohn for the Clarinet* (ABRSM)
7 **Mozart** Voi che sapete (from *The Marriage of Figaro*), arr. Benoy & Bryce. *Mozart Two Arias* (OUP)
8 **Purcell** Rondeau, arr. Richardson. *First Book of Clarinet Solos* (Faber)
9 **Reger** Romance, trans. Wastall. *First Repertoire Pieces for Clarinet* (Boosey & Hawkes)
10 **Schumann** Träumerei, Op. 15 No. 7, arr. Birtel. *Classical Highlights for Clarinet* (Schott)

LIST B

4 **Colin Cowles** The Fiery Frog Hopper's Hop: from *Amazing Animals for Clarinet* (Fentone)
5 **Fields & McHugh** On the Sunny Side of the Street, arr. Iveson (*observing lower line in bb. 35–40*). *Let's Face the Music for Clarinet* (Brass Wind)
6 **Paul Harris** Andante pacifico con rubato: 3rd movt from *Sonatina for Clarinet* (Fentone)
7 **Joplin** Maple Leaf Rag, arr. Lawrance. *Great Winners for Clarinet* (Brass Wind)
8 **John Williams** Raiders March (from *Raiders of the Lost Ark*), arr. Lawrance or arr. Galliford, Neuburg & Edmondson. *Great Winners for Clarinet* (Brass Wind) or *Ultimate Movie Instrumental Solos for Clarinet* (Alfred)
9 **Bryan Kelly** Aries: No. 1 from *Zodiac, Set 1* (Weinberger)
10 **Vinter** First Song (from *Song and Dance*). *First Repertoire Pieces for Clarinet* (Boosey & Hawkes)

LIST C

4 **Demnitz** Study in D: P. 15 No. 5 from *Elementary School for Clarinet* (Peters)
5 **Langey** Study in B minor. No. 33 from *More Graded Studies for Clarinet, Book 1* (Faber)
6 **Nilia Velázquez** Study in G minor. No. 38 from *More Graded Studies for Clarinet, Book 1* (Faber)
7 **Roger Purcell** Come What May: No. 26 from *Scaling the Heights* (Astute Music)
8 **James Rae** Exhibit A: No. 23 from *38 More Modern Studies for Solo Clarinet* (Universal)
9 **James Rae** Save As… or Polka Dotcom. *Double Click!! for Solo Clarinet* (Gumbles Publications)
10 **Philip Sparke** Ursa Major *or* Hungarian Dance: No. 37 *or* No. 38 from *Skilful Studies for Clarinet* (Anglo Music)

First published in 2017 by ABRSM (Publishing) Ltd,
a wholly owned subsidiary of ABRSM, 4 London Wall Place,
London EC2Y 5AU, United Kingdom
© 2017 by The Associated Board of the Royal Schools of Music
Distributed worldwide by Oxford University Press

Music origination by Julia Bovee and Katie Johnston (Sight-reading)
Cover by Kate Benjamin & Andy Potts
Printed in England by Page Bros (Norwich) Ltd,
on materials from sustainable sources.

With the New Guard

Avec la garde montante

Children's Chorus from *Carmen*, Act I

Arranged by Alan Bullard

Georges Bizet
(1838–75)

Bizet's *Carmen* is one of the most popular operas of all time, thanks to its memorable melodies. Although sung in French, this passionate drama is set in sunny, southern Spain and centres around two main characters: Carmen, a gypsy who works in a cigarette factory and is always getting into trouble; and Don José, the ill-fated soldier who falls in love with her.

This piece appears near the start of the opera and is sung by a children's chorus, announcing the arrival of the new guard. In bars 33–48 they sing 'tarata, tarata ta!' which are the syllables for, and fit the rhythm of, bars 33–34. The music has a strong military quality, with a sense of proud, confident marching throughout.

© 2017 by The Associated Board of the Royal Schools of Music

AB 3861a

Fantasy Piece

No. 1 from *Fantasiestücke*, Op. 43

A:2

Edited by David Blackwell

N. W. Gade
(1817–90)

Born in Copenhagen, Gade was one of the most important Danish musicians of the 19th century. Schumann was a principal influence on Gade's music, as is clearly evident in his Fantasy Pieces – a genre that Schumann himself invented. The first of Gade's Fantasy Pieces relies on a wide dynamic range for expression, almost always by gradation (*crescendo/diminuendo*) rather than sudden shifts. The gently playful triplets (bars 9–10 and 37–38) anticipate the more passionate succession of triplets in bars 47–48 – the emotional climax of the piece. **In the exam, the grace notes in the clarinet part are optional.** Although the published metronome marking is ♩ = *c*.88, you might prefer a slightly faster tempo of ♩ = *c*.104.

Source: *Fantasiestücke* (Leipzig: Fr. Kistner, 1864). A number of inconsistencies in dynamics and articulation have been corrected here without comment.

Good Luck to the Bride and Groom

Choson Kale Mazel Tov

A:3

Arranged by Franklyn Gellnick

Trad. Klezmer

Klezmer is a musical tradition of Ashkenazi Jews from Eastern Europe. Several composers have been influenced by the style, such as Mahler, who integrated it into his First Symphony. Klezmer music is generally used to accompany dancing at celebrations such as weddings, and this piece is a cheerful dance wishing good luck to a newly married couple.

The music's folk-like nature is evoked by the grace notes in the main melody, which are best played before the beat. The tune repeats several times, with a sense of variety created by the contrasting dynamics, giving each statement of the theme a different character.

If you've never heard Klezmer before, you might like to listen to recordings by Giora Feidman, one of the most famous Klezmer clarinettists.

The Wizard

from *Mr Benn* for Clarinet

B:1

Duncan Lamont
(born 1931)

Mr Benn was a favourite children's character, appearing in books and cartoons in the 1970s. In each episode he visits a fancy-dress shop and goes through a magic door, which leads him to a different world according to whichever costume he is wearing.

In this piece, Mr Benn is trying his hand at being a wizard; perhaps each musical phrase represents him casting a spell with his magic wand. The legato triplets might reflect each movement of his wrist, contrasting with the detached pairs of swung quavers. The dynamic contrasts might suggest that sometimes Mr Benn is confident with his magic skills (bar 2), but at other times (bar 16), he's rather shy!

B:2

School's Out!

First movement from *Tom Sawyer Suite*

Piano part edited
by Julius Mattfeld

James Collis
(1900–1961)

Tom Sawyer, a boy about 12 years old, is the main character in a series of novels by the American writer Mark Twain, and this music comes from a suite of pieces inspired by Tom's adventures.

'School's Out!' is all about the summer holidays, as shown through the joyful 'Hurray!' above bar 1 (don't shout this!). This carefree feeling, as if running though a forest on a sunny day, is reflected in the staccato notes of the main theme from bar 9. Perhaps the series of hairpin dynamics represent Tom racing up and down several little hills before reaching the soft conclusion, as he makes it back home.

B:3

Cooling Breeze

Christopher Norton
(born 1953)

When it's summertime and the heat of the sun is beating down, there's nothing like a nice breeze to help cool you down. The legato phrases and syncopated rhythms in this piece help to create a relaxed mood. The dynamics generally swell up and down, just as a breeze comes and goes gradually. Only in bar 17 is there a sudden shift (**mf**), marking a new section that builds up to the loudest passage, suggesting a strong gust of wind. After this climax, from bar 29 to the end, there's a sense of the music slowly winding down, gently becoming softer and softer, as the sun sets on another day.

Christopher Norton is a composer and educationalist who has written stage musicals, ballet scores and orchestral music, as well as jingles and signature tunes for TV and radio.

Dog, Bone, Mayhem

Howard Goodall
(born 1958)

If you know the nursery rhyme 'This Old Man', you'll be familiar with the line 'give the dog a bone'. This music suggests the opposite: you shouldn't give the dog a bone, as the result is mayhem! It's a piece you can really have fun with – especially the stamping! **In the exam, the stamping is optional.** However the key element is articulation: staccato and tenuto notes, legato lines, accents at the beginning and end of phrases – all these contribute to portraying the character of the playful dog.

Howard Goodall became famous through his popular TV themes, including *Blackadder*, *Mr Bean* and *QI*, and he is also known for his work as a presenter on the UK radio station Classic FM.

© 2006 by Faber Music Ltd
Reproduced from *Fingerprints – Clarinet and Piano* by permission of the publishers.
All rights reserved.

Who's Afraid of the Big Bad Pike?

C:2

No. 3 from *Fishy Scaley Studies*

Mark Nightingale
(born 1967)

'Who's afraid of the Big Bad Wolf?' is a well-known song from the tale of *The Three Little Pigs*. In this piece, Mark Nightingale has substituted the wolf for something a little more fishy: it's big with sharp teeth, and it sometimes hunts in packs like wolves: the pike! This is a hunting march with a military feel about it, especially in the middle section with the series of repeated, accented notes (bars 9–16). Try emphasising this marching character further, with cleanly detached quavers and semiquavers. Although the published metronome marking is ♩ = *c*.112, you might prefer a slightly slower tempo of ♩ = *c*.104.

Mark Nightingale is a jazz trombonist whose experience includes directing the BBC Big Band and working with such famous jazz artists as John Dankworth and Cleo Laine.

AB 3861a

C:3

Andantino in A minor

No. 63 from *Kleine theoretisch-praktische Clarinettenschule*

F. L. Schubert
(1804–68)

Franz Ludwig Schubert (not to be confused with the much more famous Franz Schubert) was a composer, pianist and music teacher, who wrote many musical exercises for both the piano and the clarinet.

This piece is taken from his *Kleine theoretisch-praktische Clarinettenschule* (Little Theoretical and Practical Clarinet School). A key feature of this piece is its wide dynamic range (from *p* to *f* and a number of hairpin swells up and down). Also, the tempo varies frequently, with three instances of slowing down, interrupting the sense of pulse. A third feature is the articulation, alternating between legato and staccato within the same phrase.

Source: *Kleine theoretisch-praktische Clarinettenschule*, herausgegeben von F. L. Schubert (Leipzig: Merseburger, n. d.). The slur in bars 2–3 is an editorial addition. The articulation in bars 23–24 has been amended to match bars 5–6.

Scales and arpeggios

SCALES

from memory
tongued *and* slurred

to a twelfth ♩ = 72

Eb major

C minor melodic

or

C minor harmonic

two octaves ♩ = 72

F major

A major

C major

D major

Scales and arpeggios

ARPEGGIOS

from memory
tongued and slurred

DOMINANT SEVENTH

from memory
resolving on the tonic
tongued *and* slurred

two octaves   ♩ = 54

CHROMATIC SCALE

from memory
tongued *and* slurred

two octaves   ♩ = 72

Sight-reading

Sight-reading

Sight-reading

Sight-reading